#1 NEW FRIENDS

#1 NEW FRIENDS

Dorothy Haas

Illustrated by Jeffrey Lindbergh

A
LITTLE APPLE
PAPERBACK

SCHOLASTIC INC.
New York Toronto London Auckland Sydney

*Dedicated to the several
Miss Krafts in my life —
teachers who made a difference.*

ISBN 0-590-41506-9

12 11 10 9 8 7 6 5 4 3 2 1   8 9/8 0 1 2 3/9

Printed in the U.S.A.   11

First Scholastic printing, July 1988

Contents

CHAPTER 1

A long yellow moving van sat in the dark street outside the red brick house in Minneapolis. It was locked up tight, waiting for morning. Then it would carry away the Buttermans' belongings.

Inside the house, behind the white shutters and the shiny green door, Polly Butterman and her best friend, Regan, sat on the floor in front of the fireplace. The living room was almost empty. Their voices echoed, even though they spoke softly.

"Remember how much fun we had at the fair?" said Polly.

1

"The Ferris wheel was spooky when it stopped when we were on top," said Regan. "And remember Chris's birthday party the day before?"

Polly giggled. "She got five sets of Magic Markers."

"Oh, Peanut," Regan said sadly, "I wish you didn't have to move away."

"Mom says we've got to go, to be near my grandpa and grandma," said Polly.

"We'll probably never see each other again," murmured Regan, watching the darting flames in the fireplace.

"Probably," Polly agreed. She sighed. "No more fairs."

"No more birthday parties," moaned Regan.

"No more walking to school together," said Polly. "No more — "

"What a pair of gloomy Gerties!" said Mrs. Butterman. She was sitting in the only chair left in the living room, writing a list. "Of course you are going to see each other. You'll visit each other. And you'll write letters. And — "

The doorbell chimed. Polly scrambled to her feet. "I'll get it. I bet it's Joe coming for Ceci."

She ran to the door and opened it to the tallest boy in the world. "Hi, Joe," she said, looking up, up, up at him. "Come on in. Ceci must be ready. She's been in the bathroom for nineteen hours.

"Ceci?" she shouted up the stairway. "Joe is here for you."

Mrs. Butterman covered her eyes with her hand. "Polly," she groaned, "that's not the way to do things. Run upstairs and quietly tell your sister that Joe has come."

Polly bounded up the stairs. Behind her, Mrs. Butterman was talking to Joe. "Come in, Joe. Promise me you'll have Ceci home by eleven."

What difference did it make, Polly wondered, whether you called upstairs about somebody coming? It sure did save a lot of walking around. And anyway, Ceci must have heard the door chimes. She must know Joe had come. So why did somebody have to go upstairs and tell her so?

Ceci's door was closed. Polly knocked and opened it. "Joe's downstairs," she said. Then, staring at her sister, she said, "Wow!"

Ceci was wearing a new yellow sweater that looked perfect with her best jeans. She had tied a yellow scarf around her hair, and she was wearing six bangle bracelets. Ceci was fifteen and gorgeous. Polly hoped she would be exactly like Ceci when she got to be fifteen.

Ceci smiled and her dimples showed. "Like it?" she asked, twirling around. "I've been saving my baby-sitting money for it for weeks."

"Wow!" Polly said again. "Can I wear it sometime? I mean, after it gets old," she added quickly.

"We'll see," said Ceci. She picked up her jacket and turned off the lamp.

"Ce?" Polly asked, following her to the door. "Are you going to kiss Joe good-bye? I mean, because we're moving away and all?"

Ceci looked shocked. In the light from the hall, her cheeks were pink. "Polly Butterman! You just don't ask questions like that!"

There. She'd done it again. What was so

wrong with asking your very own sister if she was going to kiss a boy? Polly was never going to understand what you could or could not say. Or when to yell up the stairs or not yell.

Growing up sure was full of things to learn.

She followed Ceci into the hall. Halfway down the stairs, Ceci turned and gave Polly a quick squeeze. "You're okay, Peanut. Now look after Mom tonight. Make her laugh."

"I always make her laugh," said Polly.

"You're right about that," said Ceci, smiling. "You make all of us laugh."

After Ceci and Joe left, Mrs. Butterman telephoned the Pizza Works to have a pizza delivered. Polly and Regan crowded around her at the phone.

"No mushrooms!" Polly said firmly.

"But onions?" asked Regan. "Can we have onions on it?"

"And sausage," said Polly, licking her lips. She loved pizza.

"We'll eat on the floor in front of the fire," said Mrs. Butterman after she hung up. "Why don't you girls bring the things we'll need from the kitchen. Everything's on the cabinet next to the sink," she called after them as they raced out of the living room.

The house sounded funny, Polly thought as they ran through the dining room. With no tables or chairs in them, the rooms echoed hollowly. She had never seen her house this way. It was as though the house were waiting for its people to go away.

"Look," said Regan as they gathered up paper napkins and plastic cups. She held up a bag of marshmallows. "We can toast these."

"And make S'mores," squealed Polly. "There are chocolate bars here, too. And graham crackers."

They grinned at each other. S'mores were what they made for dessert when they went camping.

Mrs. Butterman took the pizza from the deliveryman and set it on the hearth. She cut it into slices. "This is huge," she said. "Surely we won't eat it all. There'll be some left for Maggie. She will be hungry when she gets home from the game."

Polly's sister Maggie was twelve. Sometimes

6

she seemed to think she was fifteen and tried to do all the things that Ceci did. But sometimes she acted as if she were two! Maggie was a terrible trial to Polly.

They sat on the floor in front of the fire and ate the pizza — which had plenty of Italian sausage and lots of onions and no mushrooms.

"Do you think they have pizza in Illinois?" Polly patted her stomach. "I don't think I could live without pizza."

Mrs. Butterman smiled wryly. "It wouldn't surprise me if they did. Do you know — I'll bet they've even got electric lights and running water."

Later they toasted the marshmallows until they were deliciously gooey and put them between graham crackers and chocolate.

"It's terrible that something that tastes so yummy makes you so messy," said Regan, scrubbing at her face with a napkin.

"And it's terrible that something that looks so good when you begin to eat looks" — Polly made a face at the nearly empty pizza box — "so unwelcome when you're finished eating."

They carried things to the kitchen then and dumped the crumpled napkins and plastic cups into a trash carton. There wasn't even a wastebasket left in the house.

After they cleaned up the pizza mess, Polly and her mother walked Regan home. The night air felt cool, damp, and soothing on Polly's cheeks. She hardly ever got to be outdoors at night.

"Will you see the same stars I see?" Regan asked, looking up at the bright points of light in the dark sky.

Polly wasn't sure.

"Girls," said Mrs. Butterman, "we aren't moving to Australia! Of course you'll see the same stars — the Big Dipper and the North Star and all of them."

Regan flung her arms around Polly when they got to her house. "Oh, Peanut," she said in a choked-sounding voice, "I'm going to miss you so much. Halverson School isn't going to be any fun anymore."

Polly's eyes filled and she hugged Regan back. "And I have to go to that new school

and you won't be there. But I'll write to you on the stationery you gave me. I'll write as soon as I get there."

The door opened. Regan's father stood in the bright square of light. Regan gave Polly another hug and ran to him. Together, they stood in the doorway and waved good-bye to Polly.

And Polly wondered: Whenever was she going to get to talk to Regan again. . . ?

CHAPTER 2

■▀■▀■▀■▀■▀■▀■▀■▀■▀■

"Mom," said Polly as they turned toward home, "if Daddy was still here, would we have to move away?"

Her mother was quiet for a moment. Then she said, "Remember when we went to Colorado on vacation? And we went on that trail ride? And what happened?"

What did the vacation have to do with Polly's question? Grown-ups surely did go about answering things in funny ways. But — "I fell off the horse," said Polly.

"Right," said her mother. "And then what did you do?"

"Climbed back on again." Polly laughed. "I didn't think I wanted to, but I did."

"You climbed on," said Mrs. Butterman, "and we went ahead and we had a wonderful ride in the mountains. Remember?"

Polly did. "We ate from a chuck wagon. And I saw some beavers. And I yodeled."

"Right," said her mother. "We went ahead with the trail ride. Well, when someone you love dies, it's a little like climbing back on the horse and going ahead with things. Even when you don't feel like it. And sometimes good things happen."

Polly thought about that for a while. At last, looking up at the stars, she said, "But why did Daddy have to die?"

Mrs. Butterman answered slowly. "Because he was very sick. And he couldn't get well. And . . . oh, I guess God just wanted a lawyer around to talk to."

"Oh." Polly thought about that, too. "I miss him," she said at last.

"I do, too, honey," said her mother. "I do, too."

They walked the rest of the way home without talking. Mrs. Butterman held Polly's hand. Polly hadn't gone walking . . . holding her mother's hand . . . for years and years. That was for little kids. But she liked it tonight.

Maggie still wasn't home when they got there. Mrs. Butterman looked at her watch. "She doesn't really have to be here until nine o'clock, so I guess I'll put off worrying for a while."

Polly remembered the leftover pizza in the kitchen. Walking in the night air had made her hungry. "Maybe we should have another piece of pizza," she said thoughtfully. "Maybe Maggie won't be hungry and it'll just go to waste."

"Don't be greedy," said Mrs. Butterman. "Do you want to grow up greedy?"

"Yes!" said Polly, smacking her lips, her eyes dancing.

"Well, I won't let you," said Mrs. Butterman, laughing. "Now run and get ready for bed. Call me when you're ready. We'll read our book."

Polly started up the stairs, still thinking about the pizza.

"Polly?"

She looked back at her mother standing in the empty living room.

"You know," said Mrs. Butterman, "I'd kind of like company tonight. Want to sleep in my bed?"

Polly whooped. She loved sleeping in her mother's big bed. She ran upstairs to the room she shared with Maggie and leaped into her pajamas. "I'm almost ready," she yelled as she raced to the bathroom to brush her teeth.

She was sitting in the middle of the bed, making it bounce, when her mother came into the bedroom.

They read from *Winnie-the-Pooh*. Polly was really too grown-up for that book, and she never read it by herself. But it was fun when her mother read it because Mrs. Butterman laughed so hard she could hardly keep reading, and then Polly laughed, too.

They read the part about Pooh going to visit Rabbit and getting stuck in the front door after he ate too much. The last thing Polly heard was about Pooh not being able to eat for a week so he would get skinny.

Sunlight on her face awakened Polly the next morning. At first she didn't know where she was. The bed didn't feel like her bunk bed. Then she remembered and opened her eyes and yawned and stretched.

Her arm touched something papery on the pillow. She reached for it.

It was a picture of her and Daddy when she was really small. She was sitting on his lap and they were laughing and she was wearing new shoes. She remembered those shoes. They were red.

After she got dressed, she slid the picture inside the Pooh book so she would know where to find it again. She put the book and her pajamas in her backpack with the clean clothes her mother had packed for her.

Everybody was standing around the kitchen eating cereal out of paper bowls when Polly got downstairs. Ceci looked gloomy and Maggie looked as if she were still asleep. They didn't talk.

Aunt Jean came over while they were eating. She would lock up the house when the movers were through, she said. Mrs. Butterman didn't have to worry about a thing.

Loud bumping noises came from the living room. The movers were carrying the beds downstairs and out to the van.

"Okay, gang — let's get moving," said Mrs. Butterman. "You've got clean clothes for the next couple of days? Check your bags — although I don't know what we'll do at this point if you haven't packed them! But don't forget your toothbrushes."

They were all in the yard getting into the station wagon when Joe came by. He and Ceci walked back indoors.

"Don't be long," Mrs. Butterman called after them. "We're getting a late start."

"I think I forgot something," said Polly, hopping out of the car. "I'd better look in the house."

"I think you haven't and I think you'd better not," said Mrs. Butterman, her hand on Polly's shoulder. "I checked your room."

So Polly had to get back in the car, and she

didn't get to see Ceci and Joe say good-bye. How was she ever going to find out about such things if she couldn't look and Ceci wouldn't tell her?

Ceci came back to the car in a few minutes. Her eyes were pink.

Mrs. Butterman started the car and backed out of the driveway. Aunt Jean waved and waved. But Joe didn't wave or anything. He just stood by the lilac bush, by himself, looking as though he was never going to smile again.

It was very quiet inside the car. Polly sat up front with her mother. Ceci and Maggie sat in back.

After a while Mrs. Butterman slid a cassette into the tape player. A song they all liked filled the car. She began to sing. "Doe — a deer, a female deer. . . . "

Polly joined in. "Ray — a drop of golden sun. . . . "

Pretty soon Maggie and Ceci started to sing, too. When they turned onto the interstate, they were all singing. "Seventy-six trombones led the big parade. . . . "

CHAPTER
3

Polly moaned and clutched her stomach. "Isn't there even a cracker to eat in this car? I'm dying. I'm starving to death." It felt like a year and a half since they had stood around the kitchen eating cornflakes out of paper bowls.

Her mother didn't even send a kind look her way. "We'll stop for lunch in a while," she said mildly.

A while? How could her mother be so heartless? Polly remembered something. "Was there any of that pizza left from last night? Did you bring it?"

"There wasn't. I didn't," said Mrs. Butterman, speeding up to pass a truckload of logs.

Polly swung around. "You ate all the rest of the pizza!" she said accusingly to Maggie.

Maggie made a face at her. "There wasn't all that much. You really pigged out before I got home. Oink," she added, crossing her eyes at Polly.

"Double oink to you," said Polly.

Mrs. Butterman sighed. "No bickering. I guess it really is time for lunch when you all get so crabby. Start looking for a roadside rest stop."

They had been driving for what seemed like hours.

Polly studied the road map. She measured it with her hand. "We've still got almost ten inches to go. How far is ten inches?"

"A long way," said Mrs. Butterman, stretching out the *long*. "We won't get to Grandpa's until late tonight. You'll probably be sound asleep."

"There's a sign," Maggie yelled from the backseat. " 'Picnic area ahead — one half mile.' "

"Keep to the right, Mom," said Ceci.

"Don't miss it, Mom," pleaded Polly. Her stomach couldn't stand it if they had to wait for another picnic area. "There it is, there it is," she said, bouncing up and down when she spotted the turnoff ahead.

Mrs. Butterman slowed the car at the turnoff and drove into a grove of yellow-leaved trees. "Beautiful," she sighed as she stopped the car. "It looks like all the sunlight in the world is trapped right here."

Polly piled out of the car and followed her mother around to the back. "Look," she said, pointing in among the trees. "There's a fireplace. Maybe we can roast some hot dogs? And make some S'mores?"

Mrs. Butterman opened the tailgate and pulled out a carton. "Take the picnic things to that table over there. We won't need to cook, I'm sure. Aunt Jean just wouldn't do that to me."

Polly ran with the carton. She pulled a red-checked tablecloth out of the box and spread it out on the table. Then she dug out plastic cups, forks, and spoons and started placing them around on the cloth.

She never remembered later what made her look under the table. Maybe a noise drew her eyes there. But look down she did. Lying in the shadows was a tangle of hair — black, white, tawny. Jet-black eyes looked up at her from the tangle, watching her every movement.

Polly dropped to her knees and crawled under the bench. "Well, hi, pup," she said softly, holding out her hand palm up so the mop of uncombed hair could sniff it. "What are you doing here?"

She pulled back her hand when the bundle of fur let out a soft puppy growl.

The little dog didn't look especially unfriendly. But without moving, it let her know it didn't want to be touched.

Polly sat back on her heels.

"What's under here?" asked Maggie, sliding off the bench and hunkering down next to Polly. "Hey! A dog!" She reached toward it.

The puppy's growl was louder this time, as fierce as a puppy's growl can be.

"Okay already," said Maggie, withdrawing her hand. "There's nothing to be mad about!"

"What's going on?" asked Mrs. Butterman, setting the cooler on the table.

"Mom, look," Polly breathed in awe. "There's a little dog here. And there isn't another car around here anywhere. I wonder where he came from?"

Mrs. Butterman knelt, studying the little dog. "Ceci," she said over her shoulder. "Pour some water onto one of the plastic plates. Not too much," she added.

She took the plate and pushed it near the puppy.

The puppy didn't even sniff at the plate. He lapped up the water thirstily, making noisy, slurping sounds.

Ceci's eyes were round. "I wonder how long it's been since he's had water," she said. "I wonder how long he's been here."

Mrs. Butterman poured more water onto the plate. "Polly," she said softly, "pour a little milk onto a plate. See if you can warm it up by holding it in your hands."

Polly got the milk out of the cooler and poured a puddle onto a plate. She held the plate flat on her hands to warm it, and blew on it, too, to help take away the chill.

She started to slide it toward the puppy.

"No," Mrs. Butterman said sharply. "Don't get too close to him. I'd rather he nipped at me than at you." She nudged the plate toward the puppy.

He watched her, his eyes bright. But he didn't make any growling noises. And when the plate was near, he lapped at the milk hungrily.

They knelt on the grass, their own lunch forgotten, watching the little dog. When he finished drinking the milk, he gave a single weak wave of his tail.

"Well, his tail isn't broken, anyway," said Polly.

The puppy's eyes closed.

"He isn't — Oh, he isn't dead, is he?" asked Polly, alarmed.

Mrs. Butterman laid a hand lightly on the dog's back. "He's sleeping," she said. "I can feel him breathing."

Polly reached out. "He needs a good petting."

"No!" her mother said. "Let him sleep."

So Polly knelt there, her hands knotted into fists to keep them away from the puppy. She did so want to hold him.

At last they got up and went about their own lunch. But first Mrs. Butterman made everyone scrub their hands with soapy washcloths she had brought from home. "The puppy's probably all right," she said. "But then again . . . he looks so weak . . . he may be sick. Never touch an animal that's acting unfriendly."

Polly peeked under the table. Surely the puppy wasn't sick! All he needed was some water and something to eat and somebody to play with him.

It was fun to explore the lunch basket and find Aunt Jean's surprises. There were tuna salad sandwiches, small bags of potato chips, deviled eggs, pickles, raisin and carrot salad, and apples so shiny Polly saw her nose reflected in the one she bit into.

As they ate, she kept looking under the table at the sleepy bundle of fur. He didn't open his eyes.

She forgot about the puppy, though, at her

first taste of one of Aunt Jean's double-choc-olate brownies. She closed her eyes in pleasure. One of those brownies was to die for! She licked her lips and burped.

"Polly!" exclaimed her mother.

"Gross!" said Maggie, rolling her eyes.

"Come on, Peanut," said Ceci. "Girls just don't do that!"

"But what do you do if you've just got to burp?" wailed Polly. "You're always telling me what I'm not supposed to do, but nobody tells me what I should do, instead." Then she thought of something. She grinned. "My, but that did feel good."

Everyone groaned.

"She's hopeless, Ma," complained Maggie. "In that new place, I'm going to tell people she's not really my sister — we found her in a garbage can."

Polly always turned off her ears when Maggie complained. She looked down and saw the little dog moving. He was coming toward her on wobbly legs.

"Mom," she gasped. "Look. He can walk.

26

And he's wagging his tail — he's not un-friendly. He can't be sick!"

The puppy toppled over. Then he pushed himself to his feet and kept coming. He stopped when he got to Polly, fell over again, and with his head on her shoe, closed his eyes.

"Awww," Polly sighed. She didn't move her foot. She looked around. "This puppy likes me best of everyone here. He doesn't care if I burp."

And just to show them, she burped again. The puppy slept on.

CHAPTER
4

■▀■▀■▀■▀■▀■▀■▀■▀■▀■▀■▀■▀■

"Mom," Polly said desperately, "he likes me. He put his head on my foot — not anybody else's. We can't just leave him here."

They were packing up the lunch things. Mrs. Butterman was worried. "Honey, we still have a very long drive ahead of us. Grandpa and Grandma are expecting us tonight. We haven't the time or the things we need to care for a sick animal."

Polly looked around the golden grove. Leaves fluttered down with every stirring breeze. It was a beautiful place. But nobody had driven in while they ate lunch. Probably nobody was going to come here again until next summer vacation. "Whoever left him here — they aren't coming back for him," she said.

"He's been here a long time, Mom," said Ceci. "I mean, to be so thirsty and starved."

"We can't just go away, even if we do leave him some food and water," said Maggie. "Mom — you're mean!"

"He'll be scared," said Polly. "Maybe some big animal will get him. Maybe he'll just die." She couldn't help it. Her eyes filled with tears.

Mrs. Butterman rubbed her forehead, thinking. "Here's what we'll do," she said at last. "We'll take the puppy to the next town and leave him with a veterinarian. I'll pay for his care and when he's well the vet can find a good home for him."

And that's the most she would promise.

Ceci took all the lunch things — the tablecloth and plastic cups and spoons — out of the carton and stuffed them into a plastic bag.

Maggie got an old bath towel out of the car.

Polly bunched it up into the carton to make a soft bed.

The puppy whimpered when Mrs. Butterman picked him up. But he didn't growl. Gently she put him into the carton. "Put the box on the floor in back," she said, "not on the backseat. If we stop suddenly, it would slide off the seat."

When they drove away from the picnic grove, Ceci sat in front with Mrs. Butterman, and Polly and Maggie were in back. Polly curled on the floor beside the carton. "Don't be scared, fellow," she whispered. "You're going to be all right."

The puppy looked up at her out of ebony eyes that seemed to say, "I trust you."

Polly didn't see any of the red and gold and orange trees along the way, or the white birches and dark evergreens set in among them. She just watched the puppy sleep. From time to time, she touched him. Yes, he was still breathing.

The car slowed and pulled off the highway. Gravel crunched under the tires. Polly scrambled to her knees and looked out the window. They had stopped in front of a restaurant.

Mrs. Butterman opened the door on the

driver's side. "Stay here," she told them. "I'm going to look up the name of a vet and find out how to get there."

Ceci leaned over the front seat and stroked the puppy with a finger. "How's he doing?"

Polly looked up at her. "Ce, we just can't leave him somewhere. He's mine. I was meant to find him."

Trouble showed on Ceci's face. "I know, Peanut. I feel the same way. But Mom's got a lot on her mind these days. We've got to remember that."

"Clean him up and comb his hair, and I bet he'd be the cutest dog anywhere," said Maggie.

"I'll wonder my whole life about him if we just leave him with some old veterinarian," said Polly. She had never wanted anything so much in her whole life as she wanted this straggly, stray puppy.

The puppy stirred. He opened his eyes, opened his mouth, and yawned, showing his red tongue.

"I'll see what I can do," said Ceci. "I mean, I'll try talking to Mom. But I don't promise anything. Hey, I bet he could use some more water."

31

"I'll get it," said Maggie, climbing over the seat to reach the cooler.

They were all on their knees in the backseat watching the puppy when Mrs. Butterman returned. She looked at them silently for a long moment, then said, "There's a good vet in town. You won't believe this. His name is Dr. Baer."

Nobody laughed.

"Let's go," she said. "This is all taking so much time. We'll never make it to Grandpa's tonight if we don't keep moving."

They drove into town and found Dr. Baer's office on a quiet side street. Mrs. Butterman parked the car in the lot and carried the box with the puppy. The girls trailed after her.

Dr. Baer seemed to be used to emergencies. "Well, now, what have we here?" he said quietly, taking the box and leading the way to the examining room. He spoke to the puppy. "Been having a hard time, fellow?" His voice was like honey, and the little dog cocked his head at him.

They all stood around the table watching.

"Hmm," said the vet. "Hasn't had much to

eat lately, I'd say." He moved gentle fingers over the puppy. "Undernourished. Probably dehydrated." He raised his eyes to Mrs. Butterman. "This isn't your animal, is it?"

Mrs. Butterman told him the story, with Polly and the others adding the details. As they spoke, he continued his examination, moving the puppy's legs. The puppy whimpered when he touched its right foreleg.

"Could have been thrown out of a car," said Dr. Baer. "That would account for the injury to the leg. Possible fracture. I'll have to x-ray it to be sure."

Polly remembered the time she broke her arm. A broken bone hurt a lot. No wonder the puppy had growled at her when it looked like she was going to touch him. But Dr. Baer had said the puppy was undernourished, too. That meant starved.

She looked from Dr. Baer to her mother. "Is he going to be all right? He isn't going to die, is he?" Her voice shook.

The vet smiled at her. "Nothing here that food, water, and your loving him won't make right." He turned to Mrs. Butterman. "I can have him ready to travel later this afternoon. It might be best if you left him with me until tomorrow morning, though."

"Oh," said Mrs. Butterman, "that isn't what I had in mind. We still have so far to travel today. I was hoping. . . . " She went on to tell Dr. Baer her plan.

Polly took a deep breath. She couldn't stand it, never to see the puppy again. She couldn't just go away and leave him to somebody else. Somebody might love him. But somebody might be mean to him, too.

"Mom," she said.

Mrs. Butterman turned to her.

Polly plunked down on the floor. "I won't go," she said. Her lower lip stuck out. "You'll have to tie me up and carry me to the car and tie me in it and the first time you stop I'll get out and come back here."

The room was still.

Suddenly Maggie plopped down on the floor beside Polly. "Me, too," she said. "You're going to have to tie me up, too, Mom."

Mrs. Butterman looked desperately from

34

Polly to Maggie. "Now, girls," she said, "you — "

Ceci spoke. "I know I'm supposed to be grown-up and on your side, Mom. But Polly's right. We can't just leave him." Looking embarrassed, she sat down on the floor next to Polly and put an arm around her shoulders.

"Looks to me like you have a mutiny on your hands, ma'am," the vet said quietly.

Mrs. Butterman covered her eyes with her hand. "I'm whipped," she said. "I'm beaten. This is bigger than all of us. We'll keep him. We'll manage somehow."

Polly and Maggie and Ceci leaped to their feet and hugged her, all at the same time.

Dr. Baer stood by smiling.

Behind them, on the examining table, the puppy let out a soft yip.

CHAPTER
5

"My consciences," said Mrs. Butterman, looking from Polly to Maggie to Ceci. She smiled. "With you keeping me on the straight and narrow, there's no way I can ever go really wrong. Actually," her glance drifted to the puppy, "it's not sensible, but I'm glad we'll be keeping His Nibs."

"What's a Nibs?" asked Polly.

"Someone important," said Mrs. Butterman, "like a king who tells everybody what to do." She laughed wryly. "And this small dog has certainly been calling the shots today."

"He can tell me what to do anytime he wants," Polly said, grinning.

"Within reason," said Mrs. Butterman.

Ceci went back to being sort of grown-up. "I'll help with him, Mom. I'll do whatever we have to for the rest of the trip."

"So will I," said Polly. "I'll take him for his walks." She went to lean on the examining table. The puppy watched her alertly. His tail moved once. He seemed to have run out of growls.

She ran a finger over his head. "See?" she whispered. "I told you everything was going to be all right. You belong to me now, and I'm not going to let anything bad happen to you."

Maggie came to stand beside her. "He belongs to me as much as to you," she said, offering her hand to the puppy to sniff. The puppy didn't lick her fingers. Nor did he lick Polly's hand.

"He's still not very friendly," said Polly. "It's like he thinks maybe we're going to hurt him. But when he gets to our new house and he has his own bed and everything, he'll know we're his friends forever."

Behind her, Mrs. Butterman was finishing her talk with Dr. Baer. "Do what you can for him, then. We'll be back for him first thing tomorrow morning."

"Tonight, Mom?" Polly begged. "Can we come say good-night? Then he'll know we're not just going away and leaving him like those other people did."

"Not a bad idea, you know," said the vet, "for an animal that's been abandoned. I'll be here until six if you want to stop back."

And so that's what Mrs. Butterman agreed to do.

"Well," she said, settling behind the wheel of the car. "What we have to do now is find a motel. And call Grandpa." She sighed. "I hate telling him he's going to have to supervise the movers at the new house tomorrow. Well, I'll deal with that after we find a place to stay."

They drove around the little town, looking.

"A bed-and-breakfast place might be nice," Mrs. Butterman murmured.

Maggie protested. "But they never have swimming pools. Why can't we find a place with an indoor pool?"

"You haven't got a swimming suit with you," Mrs. Butterman said reasonably.

Maggie grinned. "I know you said I didn't need it. But you never know about swimming suits, when you'll need one. So I packed it just in case."

"So did I," said Ceci, laughing.

Polly was alarmed. "But I haven't got one. I mean, you packed my stuff, Mom, and I bet you didn't put my suit in there just in case."

"We'll think of something," said her mother, "if we find a place with a pool. Keep your eyes open."

They found one. The Starlight Motel had everything Polly and her sisters could have wanted.

"The pool is really big," reported Maggie, running back to the desk where Mrs. Butterman was signing them in. "It's really warm in there, and there are some palm trees in one corner."

"And it's got a sauna, too," breathed Ceci.

"And there's one of those rodeo horses you put money in and try to ride like a bucking bronco," said Polly. "It's in the hall near the

40

pool." She loved riding those mechanical horses, waving her arm like a cowboy.

Two big double beds took up most of their room. Polly went around and turned on all the lights and tried the TV. On the table between the beds was a coin box.

"What's this?" she asked. Then she read the sign on the box. MASSAGE, it said. DEPOSIT COINS FOR FIFTEEN MINUTES OF RIPPLING-MATTRESS RE-LAXING MASSAGE. "Hey, Mom," she called, "can I try this?"

"I'm going for a swim," said Maggie, dumping things out of her bag, looking for her swimsuit.

"Hold it!" Mrs. Butterman stood in the middle of the room. "Unpack your night things and your clean clothes for tomorrow. While you do that, I'll call Grandpa. Nobody leaves this room until I get that all squared away. And then I'll go with you."

"Can I talk to Grandpa first, Mom?" asked Polly. She sat on the bed while her mother put in the call. Mrs. Butterman handed her the phone while it was still ringing at the other end.

Grandpa Wayne answered.

"Poppy!" Polly blurted out. "We've got a dog. He's the neatest little guy you ever saw. Only some mean people maybe threw him out of a car. And he's got a hurt leg. And we're not coming until — "

"Slow down, Peanut." Grandpa's slow-and-easy voice cut through the rush of words. "Glad to hear you've got yourself a dog. But where are you? And what's this about not coming? Grandma's made a bucket of spaghetti sauce for dinner, and — Let me talk to your mother."

"Love you, Poppy," said Polly and handed the phone to Mrs. Butterman.

While her mother talked, Polly folded her pajamas and slid them under the pillow next to the DEPOSIT COINS box. She put *Winnie-the-Pooh* on the table under the lamp and looked closely at the picture of herself with Daddy. For the first time she saw that she was sucking her thumb in the picture. She used to do that a lot, before she grew up.

Her mother's voice trundled on in the background. " . . . probably late in the after-noon. . . . You'll keep an eye on the movers,

then? . . . Thanks, Dad. You're wonderful. . . .
Hi, Mom. . . . "

Polly curled up on the bed. How funny to
hear someone as old as your mother call her
mother "Mom." Did Mom still have to do what
her mom said? Did Nonny tell Mom about not
calling up the stairs and not burping?

"Oh, just put things where they look good.
We can move them around later. . . . No, Mom,
I won't break any speed limits. . . . " Suddenly
she held the phone out to Polly.

Polly grabbed it. "Nonny," she said, "there's
a swimming pool here, and we're going to the
vet's to say good-night to our dog at six o'clock.
That's so he'll know he belongs with us and
nobody else."

She talked to Grandma Wayne until Mrs.
Butterman made her get off the phone. "We're
not made of money, you know," she whispered.

Polly hung up, thinking about living in a
new town, Evanston, in a new house. She
hadn't thought about that since breakfast.
Regan wasn't going to be there, and she was
never going to have a best friend again. And
that new school was going to be terrible. But

she had — what had Mom called the puppy? — His Nibs. She brightened. And she was going to live right around the corner from Poppy and Nonny. That was going to be terrific.

They went down to the pool then.

Ceci was a good swimmer and did laps. Maggie was a supergood swimmer. She dove off the board and swam underwater with her eyes open. Mrs. Butterman couldn't swim, though, because she didn't have her suit. She lay in one of the long chairs under the palm trees and read a magazine.

Polly, wearing her summer shorts and her Pizza Works T-shirt, floated and dunked. When Maggie finished showing off, she helped Polly do the breaststroke at the shallow end of the pool.

"You're getting it, Peanut," Maggie said encouragingly. She sounded grown-up. "Keep working on it. You'll be a good swimmer someday."

Polly felt really good, having Maggie say a nice thing like that.

"Girls," Mrs. Butterman called after what

seemed like just two minutes, "it's time to dry off and go say sleep tight to His Nibs."

Ceci clutched at her head. "My hair! I can't go anywhere looking like this!"

Maggie looked yearningly at the diving board. "I sure would like to go off that some more."

"I'm ready," yelled Polly, climbing out of the pool, dripping water in puddles. "Let's go."

Mrs. Butterman agreed that as long as Ceci and Maggie stayed together, they could go on swimming until she and Polly got back.

Upstairs in their room, Polly toweled herself dry and got into her sweatpants and shirt. "I like the way clothes feel after I've been swimming," she said as she rubbed her hair dry, "kind of like me and them don't belong together for a while after I get dressed."

They got to Dr. Baer's at five-forty-five. He took them into his office, and there was the little dog. His leg was in a cast. But — was this the same dog they had brought here a few hours ago? Polly stood rooted to the floor, staring.

This dog's hair puffed out around him,

45

soft and fluffy. Only the black eyes peeking through the mop of fluff were the same.

"Awwww," Polly crooned. "He's the cutest dog I ever saw."

Dr. Baer laughed. "Amazing what a bath will do." He gave Polly a puppy cookie. "Here," he said. "This will tell him who his real friend is."

"His Nibs," said Polly, starting to offer it to him. She stopped. No, that didn't sound right. "Here, Nibbsie," she said, holding the cookie on her palm. "Hungry, Nibbsie?"

The puppy took the cookie daintily from her hand. He crunched it up noisily, and then he sniffed her fingers, looking for more.

Polly scratched behind his ears. "Now don't be greedy," she said. "You don't want to grow up greedy, do you?"

"Yip," said Nibbsie, nuzzling her fingers.

CHAPTER
6

The trip the next day didn't seem half as long as the morning's drive of the day before. The puppy stayed in the carton on the floor in the backseat, and Polly remained close beside him, watching him.

He gnawed on the rubber bone Dr. Baer had given him as a parting gift. But he pushed suspiciously at the red ball with the bell inside that Polly had bought for him. He seemed afraid of the tinkling sound. Then he found that the ball didn't make noise until he moved it, and he became more and more brave. At last he nosed at it and growled fiercely. The

47

red ball didn't growl back — it wasn't going to hurt him. He fell asleep with his nose against the ball.

They stopped from time to time so that he could look around at the trees. "So he'll get the idea what trees are for," said Mrs. Butterman.

Polly and Maggie took turns carrying him because he had trouble walking with the cast on his leg. They didn't mind one bit. It was a chance to hold him, and, as Polly pointed out, he needed a lot of cuddling to make up for the terrible way somebody had treated him.

Polly thought His Nibs came to her more eagerly than he went to Maggie. He was her dog. She was sure of it. Almost.

They left the puppy alone only while they stopped to eat lunch at a restaurant. Polly wanted to stay outside in the car with him, but her mother wouldn't hear of it. So — double-checking to be sure the doors were locked and that a couple of the windows were slightly open — they went into The Embers and sat in a booth next to a window where they could keep an eye on the car. When they came out, His Nibs was still there, sleeping soundly. Nobody had dognapped him.

Polly clambered into the car, making lots of noise and bumping His Nibs's box — not accidentally. He woke up and looked at her before he looked at Maggie and yipped.

Later that day Polly hoped she wouldn't have to write an essay at her new school — "My Trip from Minneapolis to Evanston." Because all she saw was the tops of trees against the blue sky and the underside of overpasses on the expressways — if she bothered to look up. Mostly, she sat on the floor and played with His Nibs.

She did pay attention when Maggie said, "We're almost there. I remember that shopping mall — what's it called . . . Old Orchard? Grandma took me there last summer to get my hair cut for my birthday. And she let me have a manicure, with any color polish I wanted — except black."

Polly pulled herself to her knees. "I remember that place," she said, pointing at a sign on a building that said Vogue Tyres. "Vo-gew-ee Tear-ees. I wonder what they are."

In the front seat, Ceci giggled.

"Shhh!" Mrs. Butterman said softly. "It's pronounced *Vohg Tires,*" she said to Polly. "Vogue means fashionable. And that's the way people in England spell tires for cars."

"I didn't know tires could be fashionable," said Polly. Then, as they headed east on Golf Road, she asked, "Do you suppose they spell 'fires' *f-y-r-e-s*? And 'wires' *w-y-r-e-s*?"

"I don't think so," said Mrs. Butterman. "Think about *so*. That can be spelled *s-o* and *s-e-w*."

"Sew — a needle pulling thread," sang Polly, a line from her favorite song.

"No — that kind of *so* is *sol*," said Ceci, who studied singing.

It took a while to get to Evanston, but when they did the trees in the streets were as red and yellow as those in Minneapolis, and when they stopped at a stoplight, Polly saw a pizza place.

"Mom," she said, hope rising in her, because it had been a long time since lunch, "do you suppose we can stop there for a snack?"

"No, I don't suppose," said Mrs. Butterman. "Dinner isn't too far off, and we're going to eat with Grandma and Grandpa."

At last they pulled to a stop in front of a rambling old house set far back on a wide lawn. A weeping willow tree filled one corner of the front yard.

"Oh, Mom! It's quaint!" breathed Ceci. "It looks like it came out of that English movie we saw last week."

"Look at all those little diamond-shaped windows," said Maggie. "There must be a room way up there under that peaky roof. Can that be mine?"

Polly didn't say anything. The front door of the house had opened. Grandma and Grandpa Wayne stepped onto the porch smiling.

"Poppy!" shrieked Polly. "Nonny!" She tumbled out of the car, cut across the lawn, leaves crackling under her feet, and was hugging them while Mrs. Butterman and Ceci were still getting out of the car.

"I thought we'd never get here, Poppy," said Polly. "We've been driving just forever."

Grandpa Wayne swung her off her feet. "I thought you'd never get here, either, Peanut. I was afraid I was going to have to eat spaghetti by myself for the next month."

"Nonny! When did you get so small?" asked Polly. "I'm almost as tall as you."

Grandma Wayne kissed her and then held her off to look at her. "Why, you've grown inches since June!"

Mrs. Butterman and the girls were coming up the walk, calling and laughing. Nobody had remembered His Nibs.

Polly raced back to the car and gathered him up. "Did you think we forgot you, Nibbsie? You're home now. This is where you live, and don't you forget it."

She carried him to the porch.

"Grandfather," she said very politely, "Grandmother, I'd like you to meet our dog. His name is His Nibs, only I call him Nibbsie. Nibbsie," she said, looking into his eyes, her finger under his chin, "I'd like you to meet my grandparents."

"What lovely manners," said Grandma

Wayne, turning to Mrs. Butterman. "Aren't you proud of her, dear?"

Behind Grandma Wayne, Maggie rolled her eyes. "You ought to hear her — "

"Margaret?" Mrs. Butterman said quietly.

Maggie didn't finish telling whatever terrible thing she was going to say about Polly.

Boxes were piled everywhere inside the house, and no curtains or draperies softened the light coming through the diamond panes of the windows. But the blue-and-white sofa sat in front of the fireplace in the living room, and there was a log ready for lighting in the grate. The statue of the shepherd girl and her lambs sat on the table below the stairs in the hall. The breakfront filled one wall in the dining room, its empty shelves waiting for the red unicorn plates that would soon stand on them.

Upstairs, Mrs. Butterman's big bed was in place in the front bedroom. Ceci's white four-poster and dresser filled one room, and Maggie and Polly's bunk beds stood waiting in another bedroom.

"Do you want me to take those apart?" asked

Grandpa Wayne. "You said something about the girls having separate rooms, but since you don't have furniture for both. . . . "

Mrs. Butterman shook her head, looking flustered. "There's so much to do here. I won't get around to furniture for Maggie's room until everything is out of boxes and put away."

"I want a waterbed," said Maggie. "I'll dream all the time that I'm swimming."

"We'll see," said Mrs. Butterman as they moved on to the rest of the house.

Polly stayed behind in the bedroom, looking around.

Windows looked out on the red leaves of a maple tree beside the house. "See that, Nibbsie?" she asked, going to look out the windows. "I bet there will be birds' nests there and we'll see them when all the leaves are gone."

She turned back to the room. "This is going to be my very own special place, as soon as Maggie gets her waterbed and stuff. Nobody can come in unless I invite them. But you can come anytime. You can sleep here. There will even be an extra bunk bed, and you can have that."

She looked down. His Nibs hadn't heard a word she said. He was sound asleep.

"Polly?" Her mother called from downstairs. "Come now. We're going to Grandma and Grandpa's for dinner. We'll sleep there to-night."

CHAPTER
7

▪▬▪▬▪▬▪▬▪▬▪▬▪▬▪▬▪

Polly had a job to do. It was the next day, and she was opening the boxes in the living room, taking out books and putting them on the shelves. There were a lot of interesting ones. How funny that she didn't remember seeing them before! She sat on a carton to look at one of the best, about a lady saving the gorillas in Africa.

"Polly!" Her mother stood in the hall outside the living room. "Have you taken Nibbsie outside in the last hour? He seems much too interested in that table leg."

"Oh, my gosh!"

Polly dropped the book, ran to the puppy, scooped him up, and got him outdoors just in time. Her mother's voice followed her. "Remember. You are to take him outside today every half hour."

"Sorry, Nibbsie," said Polly. "I started reading that book. It's terrible what happens to me when I read a book. I forget things."

She picked him up and he licked her chin. "I won't forget again," she promised. To make it up to him, she carried him around the yard, showing him every tree and bush so he would know this yard was his very own property.

"How do you expect that puppy to grow if you don't let him exercise?" asked Grandpa Wayne. He was coming up the front walk carrying his tool chest. "He won't develop his muscles if you carry him everywhere."

"Well, I know that," said Polly. "But it's really hard for him to walk with the cast on his leg." She grinned. "Look. I autographed it this morning, just like it was a people cast. So did Mom and Maggie and Ceci. Want to sign it, too?"

Grandpa Wayne tipped his head back and

looked at the names through the bottom of his glasses. "Not much room there for another name. Here. Let me take him for a minute."

Polly spilled Nibbsie into Grandpa's big hands. Grandpa moved him around, looking at him, touching the cast. "You know, Peanut, I've got an idea. Let me borrow your friend here for a while."

"What kind of an idea?" Polly wanted to know.

"You can come back to my workshop with me and see," said Grandpa Wayne, "or you can wait here and be surprised. Which will it be?"

Polly hated mysteries. She hated having to wait for things. "I'll come — " she started to say.

"Hey, Peanut!" Maggie poked her head out the front door. "Mom says you're to finish the books pronto."

Polly made a face. "I guess I'll have to wait and be surprised." She brightened. "Why don't you give me a hint? I'm a good guesser."

Grandpa set his toolbox on the porch. "Nope.

It'll have to be a surprise." He strolled down the walk, heading for home.

Polly watched him go. Suddenly something high in the air caught her attention. "Poppy!" she called. "Look up! Up there!" She ran toward him, her eyes on a giant blue balloon above the trees.

Grandpa Wayne squinted up .at it. "Well, I'll be. A hot-air balloon."

The balloon was clearing the treetops, but it was low enough for them to see that it looked like an enormous flower. A basket hung below the flower and someone was in it. Polly hopped up and down, waving wildly. The balloonist waved back.

"I never saw anything like that before," said Polly. "Things sure are different here in Evanston."

"I've been here in Evanston for a good many years," said Grandpa Wayne, "and I've never seen anything like that before."

Maggie appeared at the front door again. "Peanut, you better — "

"Maggie, look! Look!" yelled Polly, pointing.

Maggie came down the walk, her head back, staring at the amazing sight. She joined Polly and Grandpa Wayne, and together they watched the huge balloon move away on the wind.

"Oh, but it's beautiful," sighed Polly, "the way it moves, so slow . . . and . . . sort of . . . stately."

"Where did it come from?" Maggie asked in awe.

"Beats me," said Grandpa Wayne. "Maybe they'll tell about it on the TV news tonight. Watch the news."

"Can't," said Maggie. "We haven't got any electricity yet. No TV."

"Oh, the electric company will come today," said Grandpa. "Don't you fret." And he headed for home, whistling softly between his teeth.

"Poppy," Polly called after him, remembering her mother's instructions. "Mom says Nibbsie has to go outside every half hour today."

"Don't worry," Grandpa said over his shoulder. "Who do you think taught your mother about housebreaking puppies?"

Polly finished opening all the boxes and

putting away the books. First she put all the blue books together, and all the red ones, and all the yellow ones. Then she changed her mind. She ended putting all the animal books on one shelf, and all the art books on another, and all the grown-up story books on still another shelf. In time, there were no boxes on the floor in the living room and a growing mountain of empty boxes in the yard next to the back door.

"I should take you all around to your schools today," Mrs. Butterman had said that morning when they came to the new house after breakfast at Grandma's. "But that can wait until tomorrow. Today I want you here, helping turn this house into our home. By tonight I want each of your rooms ready for sleeping. And I want this living room looking like a pleasant place to relax."

Polly looked around. With the familiar furniture, with the books on the shelves, the living room did look homey.

Someone from the telephone company came that day. And then the Buttermans had a phone and a new number to remember. But there was nobody for Polly to call. And nobody to call her.

Someone from the gas company came and did something in the basement. After that they had hot water for showers and a stove to cook on.

Someone from the electric company arrived, too. Suddenly lights went on all over the house and the refrigerator began to hum. Grandma Wayne came with bags of groceries and filled the refrigerator. Polly ate an apple at once.

That afternoon, as the sun made diamond-shaped window patterns on the living room carpet, Mrs. Butterman sank into a rocking chair. "Ooof! My aching back!"

Ceci touched a match to the tinder in the fireplace and crackling sounds filled the room as tongues of fire licked at the log. "I'm going to make hot chocolate for everybody," she announced and headed for the kitchen.

Polly curled up in front of the fire with the gorilla book.

Grandma Wayne settled onto the sofa sideways, with her feet up. "It's cozy," she said, looking around. "Oh, I'm going to love having you so near."

"Where's Grandpa?" asked Maggie. "He's hardly been here all day. His tools are still out on the front porch, but — "

"He said he was making a surprise," said Polly. "I guess when he's ready he'll come — "

The ringing of the telephone filled the room.

Nobody moved. They stared at the phone as though they had never seen one before.

"Who on earth?" said Mrs. Butterman. "We don't know anyone here."

"It must be your father," said Grandma Wayne, "wanting to be the first to talk on your new phone."

Mrs. Butterman picked up the telephone. "Hello?"

She listened. A pleased smile appeared on her face. "My goodness. What a nice surprise! Imagine your getting our new number so quickly. Well, don't talk long now. Yes. Here she is. . . . "

Still smiling, she held out the phone to Polly. "It's for you, honey."

"For me?" Polly's eyes were round. Who could be calling her? . . . She took the phone. "This is Polly. . . . Regan!" she squealed. "I can't believe it's you!

"It's Regan," she hissed, looking around at everybody.

"Don't talk long," whispered Mrs. Butterman. "Remember, it's long distance."

Polly didn't hear her mother. "Oh, Regan," she burbled. "Wait till you hear. We've got a puppy, and — "

The front door opened. Grandpa Wayne came in carrying Nibbsie. He set him on the floor and the little dog came straight to Polly, running on three legs, his hurt leg in its cast rolling along on a kind of cart.

"Oh, Regan," Polly went on, "you ought to see him. He just came in. His front leg is in a cast, but my grandpa put a wheel thing on it. And do you know something? Everybody's here in this room. But" — she knelt down to hug Nibbsie — "he came straight to me."

CHAPTER 8

"Hang onto your balloons, everybody. We'll let them all go at the same time. Don't push. There's one for each of you." Mr. Granger's booming voice carried over the heads of everyone at Lighthouse Park.

Jillian looked up at her balloon. It was pink, the kind of pink people call "hot." What a neat color! A happy color! She felt the tug of the balloon on the string. She bounced her hand and watched the balloon bound around overhead.

"What are you doing, Jilly?" Emmy watched her. Then she made her own balloon bounce.

66

Erin bounced her balloon, too. So did everyone standing around Jillian. Soon the air was filled with bobbing balloons.

Nate and Ollie came running, their balloons floating straight out behind them.

"I got a green one," Nate announced, saying something that didn't need to be said because anyone could plainly see that he had a bright green balloon.

"I got a boy-colored balloon," said Ollie, looking up at his deep blue balloon. His glance drifted to Jillian's balloon. "Who'd want a girl color like that?"

Jillian pretended not to hear him. She didn't tell him there are no "boy" colors or "girl" colors — only happy colors or sad colors or feeling-noisy or feeling-quiet colors. Today was too much fun to argue with Ollie.

She turned her face up to the sky. The sun felt warm on her cheeks and the wind moved her hair. The wind pushed at her balloon, too. She watched it move around against the sky and the trees.

Even though school had begun, the trees were still green and the grass was thick and soft under her feet. Lake Michigan and the sky were so blue that they matched. Only a few puffy white clouds drifted overhead. It was a perfect day to send up the balloons and let the wind carry them away.

Nate and Ollie began a balloon fight, trying to make their balloons bump into each other.

"All right, people. Settle down," Miss Kraft called. "Oliver? Nathan? We'll launch any minute now, as soon as everyone has a balloon."

The boys bumped their balloons one more time and then stopped.

"Awwwww." The sound came from many throats.

Everyone looked. A red balloon was floating upward.

"Oh, Elvis," said Miss Kraft. "I told you to hang on to your balloon."

Elvis stood there looking rueful, his eyes on the balloon disappearing into the sky. "It escaped," he said, tucking his empty hands behind his back. Then he grinned. "Mine got a head start. It'll get somewhere first and maybe my card will come back first."

"All right now, everyone," called Mr. Granger. "We'll do the countdown together, counting backward from ten. When we get to one, we'll let the balloons go all at the same time. Ready? Ten."

"Nine," chanted Jillian. "Eight."

The voices got louder as everyone shouted the numbers. "Seven. Six. Five. Four. Three. Two. ONE!"

"Blast off!" somebody yelled as the balloons crowded upward.

Some of the balloons moved faster than others, as though they were eager to get away from the ground. They bobbed and twisted and bumped into each other. Blue, green, pink, and purple, they floated up to the treetops. A bunch of balloons that seemed to be tied together moved upward faster than the others. Several balloons, caught by a breeze, drifted toward a tree.

"Oh-oh-oh!" yelled several of the kids.

The balloons hung there for a minute, bright spots against the dark green leaves. Then

another breeze touched them and one by one they floated free, away from the tree, upward . . . upward. . . .

Jillian stood with her head back, watching. The balloons looked like colored jellybeans against the blue of the sky.

"That's it, people," boomed Mr. Granger. "Now find your teachers. Gather into class groups."

Jillian had taken her eyes off the balloons for just a minute when Mr. Granger spoke. When she looked back at the sky, the balloons were like little pinpricks. She squinted. And then the dots were completely gone.

It had all happened so fast! They had been talking and planning for a whole week, and then poof! — just like that — the balloon launch was over.

Mr. Granger was still talking. "Miss Kraft, why don't you take your third-graders over near those rocks on the shore. Mrs. Hooper, you head for the lighthouse. Mr. Moore, you and your people can sit in the playing field."

Jillian trailed after the others toward the huge rocks that kept high waves out of the park during storms. This was the first big project of the school year. In a while, the balloons would settle to earth someplace. Each balloon carried a card with a student's name on it so that whoever found it could write and tell where the balloon went down. The class that got the most cards back would keep the school flag outside their door for the rest of the month. And there were prizes, too.

"Well, Jillian," a voice boomed beside her. "Is your room going to win?"

Jillian's heart sank into her gymshoes. She didn't have to look — she knew who was walking beside her. Mr. Granger's voice could shake the walls of a brick building.

She always wanted to hide inside herself when Mr. Granger talked to her. She wanted to just dry up and disappear. But she looked up at the principal sideways from under her blonde bangs. "Yes," she whispered.

"Good," boomed Mr. Granger. "You just keep thinking that way and it may happen. And you keep thinking about getting over your shyness, too. Maybe that will happen this year. You'd like that, wouldn't you?"

Jillian felt her face get hot. Why did Mr. Granger always talk about shyness? She didn't talk to him about having a voice so loud it scared the birds right out of the trees. She had to say something, though. "Yes," she said softly.

"Good, good, good," boomed Mr. Granger.

Miss Kraft started talking about the balloon launch then, and Jillian ran to sit on a rock with Emmy and Erin. Emmy and Erin were best friends. But they made room for her to sit between them.

CHAPTER
9

Jillian burst into the house, running. The front door banged behind her. She dropped her backpack with a *thunk* on the boot-keeper-umbrella-stand-coatrack in the front hall. Then she leaned forward and studied her face in the mirror. Did she look like a shy person? Was there some terrible way a shy person looked?

Wide gray eyes returned her gaze. They said nothing at all about shyness.

A smoke-colored shadow slid around the archway and into the hall. Jillian's cat, Bumptious, jumped up onto her backpack. Jillian scooped her up. "Hi, Bumpy. Did you miss me? Hmmmm?"

"Is that you, Attila the Hunger?" Mr. Matthews's voice drifted down from his studio. "Come on up for a snack."

Jillian rubbed her chin on the little cat's silky head. "Do you think I'm shy, Bumpy? Do you care if I am?"

Bumptious flicked Jillian's chin with her rough tongue. Then she wriggled and Jillian set her down.

With Bumptious at her heels, she darted up the stairway. On the second floor, an open door showed stairs that led to the studio in the attic. She took the steps two at a time, lifting herself with her hands on the walls on either side.

Mr. Matthews was bent over his drawing table, carefully inking a piece of artwork.

"How'd you know that was me downstairs?" Jillian asked.

He didn't answer and she slipped around behind the slanted drawing board to see what he was working on. She was careful not to bump the board. If she did and he messed up a pen line, he might have to do the whole thing all over again.

"You always know," she said, her eyes on the drawing of a sofa and some chairs. Boring! She liked it best when he had a job for kids' stuff like bicycles. Or for wildlife, like ducks and bears.

Mr. Matthews didn't take his eyes off his work. "I've got X-ray eyes, that's how I knew it was you, food-face."

"Oh, Daddy!" That's all the answer she was going to get. Jillian had been trying since first grade to figure out how her father could always guess who came in downstairs when he was way up here at the top of the house.

Mr. Matthews leaned back in his chair and studied the drawing. "Yep," he said, his head tilted to one side. "Okay. That'll do it." He wiped his pen and closed the ink bottle.

Jillian poked around in the small refrigerator under the sloping roof at the front of the studio. She found jelly and fruit and milk and set them out on the low table there. She got crackers out of the tall can on the counter and glasses and a knife for the jelly out of the cabinet. Then she flopped down on one of the puffy pillows next to the table. Bumptious leaped into her lap.

Mr. Matthews came to the table, carrying his coffee cup. "Well. Did Louisa May Alcott School survive another day of you kids?"

Jillian bit into a jelly-covered cracker and told him about the balloon launch. "Everyone's wondering when the first card will come back. And where from." Then she remembered. She frowned and told him about Mr. Granger. "I don't like it when Mr. Granger says I'm shy."

Mr. Matthews sipped his coffee. "Did you tell him that?"

Jillian blinked. Tell Mr. Granger? She couldn't! Oh, she just could not!

Sounds came from downstairs.

"Think about it," said Mr. Matthews. He went to the stair rail and leaned over it. "Is that you, Mrs. Potter? Come upstairs for a cup of coffee."

"Oh, me, all those stairs," Mrs. Potter wheezed

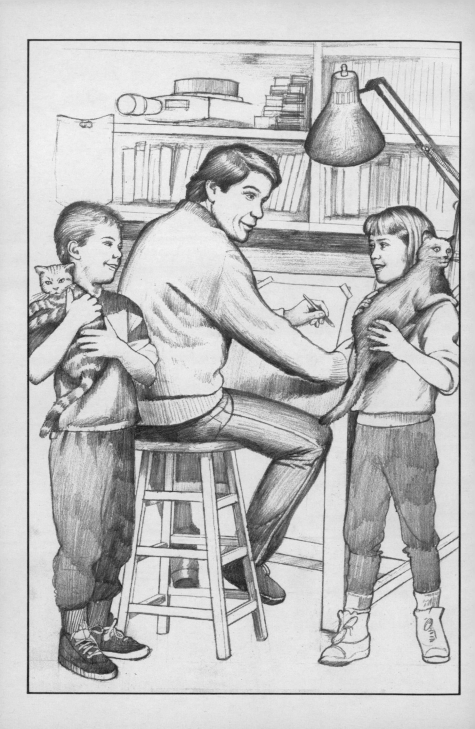

from below. "I think I'll pass for today, thank you. Jackie, you run upstairs and see your daddy now."

There was murmured talk.

"He'll be right up," Mrs. Potter called. "He's looking for Bonkers."

"Thanks for everything, Mrs. Potter," Mr. Matthews called. "See you tomorrow. Come on, Jackie old boy. You, too, Jerry."

Jackie came up the stairs one at a time. Jackie was almost five, but he was small, and stairs were still hard for him. He was clutching Bonkers, his yellow-black-and-white patched cat. Mr. Matthews leaned down for a welcome-home hug, and they came to the table together.

Jerry followed, a yellow cat draped around his neck. Jerry was twelve, and because he was oldest he seemed to think he was in charge of everybody. Sometimes he was helpful, and that was nice. But sometimes he was just plain bossy. "The water bowl down in the kitchen is empty," he said. "Doesn't anyone around here care if these cats get thirsty?"

"If it was empty," Mr. Matthews said in his easygoing way, "it's because you didn't fill it this morning. Dr. Blankenstein is your cat, and it's up to you to see that he has water to drink."

Jerry sent Jillian a look that would have turned rain into instant ice. "It was Jilly's turn."

"Wasn't," said Jillian, sending the look right back at him. "I did it yesterday."

"You owed me," said Jerry. "I did it for you last — "

"Peace!" said Mr. Matthews. "Don't take out your problems on your pets. Somebody get those animals some water."

"I've got it, Daddy." While Jerry and Jillian had argued, Jackie had gone to the sink, climbed on a stool, and filled a bowl with water. Now he was coming to the table, walking slowly, the water sloshing out of the bowl. He set it on the floor, splashing more water around. "Bonkers gets first drink."

He knelt on the floor, watching the calico cat lap at the water.

Mr. Matthews looked from Jerry to Jillian. "I hope you're feeling a little ashamed."

And for a fact, Jillian was. Jackie was such a good little kid. He just grinned at people and quietly went about his business. He never took sides. He was her friend and Jerry's, too. Sometimes she wished he would take her side because Jerry was such a prune. But she couldn't blame Jackie if he didn't.

There was a sound on the stairs. "I'm home," a soft voice sang out.

Daddy reached for a cup and filled it with coffee. "Come and have something wet."

Mrs. Matthews's head showed above the stair rail, and she came up and into the studio. "I got away from school early."

She came to the table, smiling, and kissed Mr. Matthews. Then she went around the table, dropping kisses on everybody's head. But she stopped when she looked down at Bumptious. "Kissing stops here. We're a three-cat family, but kissing's only for people."

Jillian never let her mother see her kiss Bumpy. There was no need to upset her. And Bumpy needed kissing sometimes.

Mrs. Matthews kicked off her shoes, settled

down, and rubbed her feet. She sipped her coffee. "I've got great kids this year. They are all trying so hard."

Jillian liked it when they all sat around the table and talked after school. Daddy was always here, of course, because he worked at home. Jackie got home from Mrs. Potter's early, too. But Mom didn't usually make it. She always had something to keep her at school — parent meetings, or teacher meetings, or sometimes one of her kids needed special help. They needed a lot of help because they were handicapped.

A loud slurp from across the table drew Jillian's eyes to Jerry the Prune. Weird Jerry. He was eating a pear with his head back so the juice wouldn't dribble down his chin. Jerry usually didn't get home because he had basketball practice after school. When they were all together like this, Jerry didn't give her such a hard time.

Jerry. Maybe Jerry couldn't help being weird. Maybe that's what came of having ears that stuck out like cup handles.

CHAPTER
10

Emmy and Erin were giggling. Jillian saw them as soon as she went out of the house the next morning. They were coming along the sidewalk, their heads together. Emmy was chattering and laughing, and Erin was listening and laughing. Emmy saw Jillian and waved. Jillian waited for them to catch up.

"You'll never guess what!" Emmy looked ready to explode.

"What," said Jillian, straight-faced. "There. I guessed."

Emmy looked puzzled. Then she caught on.

"Smartypants! No, I mean, I saw something yesterday afternoon after school."

"Really, Jilly," said Erin, her brown eyes dancing, "you'll never guess what she saw. Not in a billion years."

The two girls looked at Jillian eagerly, waiting.

Jillian rolled her eyes. "Come on, you guys! You don't even give a hint, and I'm supposed to guess?"

Emmy looked mysterious. "Here's a clue. It was someone from school doing the most as-ton-ish-ing thing."

When Emmy got onto one of her you'll-never-guess trips, she could hold out forever. Jillian went along with her for the moment. "You saw Mr. Granger," she said, "dressed up like a chimpanzee, sitting on the flagpole in front of the fire station, eating a banana." To add to the picture, she scratched her ribs and made her mouth round and said, "Ooh-ooh-ooh."

Emmy screeched with laughter. "Only you would think of that, Jillian Matthews. Well, you're sort of warm, about the banana. But that's only part."

"Tell her. Tell her," Erin urged, poking Emmy.

"Emmy," Jillian said softly, threateningly, "if you don't tell this minute, I'm going to tell Ollie you love him."

"You wouldn't!" Emmy gasped. "I mean, I don't love him at all."

"Tell," said Jillian. "Or I tell."

Emmy started grinning again. "Yesterday I went grocery shopping with my mom after school. We were picking out bananas and tomatoes and stuff at the Jewel and I saw Miss Kraft."

"So?" Jillian waited.

"She was with a man," said Emmy, her eyes sparkling.

Erin bubbled over with the news. "And he touched her hand. And he looked deep into her eyes, right there next to the bananas and oranges. And we think," she finished with a squeal, "he's her boyfriend."

Wow! Miss Kraft in love! "Is he handsome?"

Jillian asked. "Is he tall and dark? Has he got curly hair?"

"He's taller than she is," said Emmy. "His hair is blond like hers. Not curly. I couldn't tell what color his eyes were, though, because my mom dragged me away. She said I was being in-tru-sive. That means nosy."

Jillian sighed happily. A real love story, right before their eyes. "It'll be like *As the World Turns*," she said. And for the rest of the way to school they talked about Miss Kraft and Mr. X. That's what Erin called him — Mr. X. They were all going to watch for signs of Miss Kraft — the prettiest teacher at school — being in love.

The school day was busy. Jillian liked the art part and the reading part. She sort of liked the science part, too. Science was full of surprises. They talked about their balloons.

"Some of us guys tied our balloons together to make a big O," said Ollie. "Only they didn't go up like an O. They just went up in a big bunch."

"You should have put sticks between them to hold them apart," said David, quiet David.

David didn't talk much, but he knew an awful lot of answers to things.

Ollie swung around in his seat. "But the O wouldn't have been round then."

"You could have sort of bent the sticks," said David. "You know — made them into arcs."

"We weren't building arks," said Ollie. He laughed. "It wasn't even raining."

Everyone, almost everyone, laughed. But some of the kids looked puzzled.

"Erin," said Miss Kraft, "look up 'arc' spelled with a 'C' in the dictionary and tell us what it means. And you, Kevin, you look up 'ark' spelled with a 'K' and tell us about that."

Ollie snickered.

Miss Kraft fixed a stern eye on him. "And you, Oliver, I want you to look up 'pun.'"

"'Pun'?" said Ollie. "What kind of word is that? How do you spell it? I can't look up a word I don't know how to spell."

"P-U-N," said Miss Kraft. "Look it up and you'll find out what kind of word it is."

"Work, work, work," muttered Ollie as he followed Erin and Kevin to the big dictionary under the windows.

Miss Kraft asked why the balloons had lifted into the air, why they hadn't just stayed near the ground.

Jillian thought she knew the answer, but she didn't raise her hand. Sometimes she felt funny about knowing so many of the answers.

The kids had lots of ideas about the balloon question. But they couldn't agree on one answer.

"I think we'll divide this up into special reports," said Miss Kraft.

Everybody groaned.

"Jillian, suppose you find out all about helium. That's what filled the balloons.

"David, I want you to look up wind directions.

"Elena, you look into hot and cold air. Tell us what happens when air heats up or cools down."

She assigned reports to some of the other kids, too. Then she said they could go to the learning center one at a time. Elvis got the first library slip. He put up his hands like rabbit ears and wiggled his fingers at everyone before he closed the door.

They all talked a lot about whose cards would come back soonest, and which room was going to win the flag.

Ollie was sure they were going to win. "I just know we are," he said.

Nate wasn't so sure. "Maybe none of the cards will come back," he worried.

CHAPTER
11

It wasn't until the middle of the next week that the cards began to come in the mail. By that time everybody knew about arcs and arks and puns. They had learned about lighter-than-air helium and winds and what happens to air when it heats up or cools down.

They were just finishing with science one day when Mrs. Perrin came to the door. Mrs. Perrin was the school secretary. She handed something to Miss Kraft. When Miss Kraft closed the door and turned to the class, everyone could see she was holding postcards in her hand.

"Hey! We got some cards back," yelled Ollie.

"Whose are they? Whose are they?"

"Where did they come from?"

"Is mine there?"

Everyone crowded around Miss Kraft.

Jillian couldn't take her eyes off the cards in Miss Kraft's hand. Where had the hot-pink balloon gone down?

"Back to your seats, people," said Miss Kraft. "I'm not giving out a single one of these until you simmer down."

So they all scrambled back to their seats. But they scrambled quietly.

"That's better," said Miss Kraft. "Now, when I give you your cards, you are to stand up and read them aloud so we all can share them. Nate, this one's for you."

Nate lost his worried look. The cards were coming back! He read the card to himself first, his lips moving. Then he read it aloud. "It says here: 'Dear Nathan. I was taking my dog, Pet Rock —'"

"A dog named Pet Rock?" giggled Elvis.

"Quiet," everyone grumbled. "Let him finish."

" ' — for a walk on the beach and I found your balloon in some tall grass. Sincerely, Mrs. Trudy McCarthy, Dune Acres, Indiana.' Where's that?" he asked, looking up from the card. "I don't think Indiana touches Lake Michigan."

"It has to, Dumbo," said Ollie. "Didn't she say she was walking on the beach?"

"We'll look for it on the map in just a minute," said Miss Kraft. "But here's another card. Elena?"

"Mine?" Elena squealed. She took the card and read slowly. " 'Dear Elena. It's a good thing your card was wrapped in plastic. Your balloon was dipping into the lake when I found it. I was sailing. Good luck with your project, kiddo. Art Patrick.' "

Jillian bounced up and down with impatience. "But where on the lake? I mean, the lake is huge."

"Where did Art Patrick mail the card?" David asked quietly. "That will give us a hint."

"Can you read the postmark?" asked Miss Kraft.

Elena squinted at it. "It's blurry. Beverly Shores? MI? That means Michigan. Michigan's farther away than Indiana, I think." She looked pleased.

And so that was another place to look up on the map. And they had to look up Kalamazoo, MI, too. That's where Courtney's card came from.

But Jillian's card did not come back that day.

As they were looking at the places on the map, she thought of something. Mr. Moore's class had received two cards yesterday, and Mrs. Hooper's class got three. Miss Kraft's class was at the bottom. Zero.

"I wonder how many cards the other classes got back today?" Jillian wondered aloud.

They went out into the hall to look at the balloon-ometers.

The balloon-ometers were like thermome-ters. Only they were made of cardboard and each one had a balloon on a stick at the top. There was a place on the balloon-ometers for marking how many cards each class got back.

The red line on Mr. Moore's balloon-ometer was still at 2. But the red line on Mrs. Hooper's balloon-ometer had gone up to 4.

Jillian was class artist. It was her job to mark their balloon-ometer. She got down on her knees and with her red Magic Marker began coloring the balloon-ometer from the bottom up to 3.

A booming voice spoke while Jillian was coloring. "Well, I see we're beginning to get results," said Mr. Granger. "It looks to me like Mrs. Hooper's class is ahead."

Oh, but we'll catch up. There's lots of time yet, thought Jillian. But she didn't say it aloud.

Ollie spoke up. "Aw, we're only one card behind. We're going to beat everyone. We're going to win the flag."

"You just keep up your enthusiasm," Mr. Granger boomed as he headed back to his office.

"If we win the flag," Jillian said to her father that afternoon, "we all get free ice-cream cones from 31 Flavors."

"I see. Food. That should suit you just fine, food-face," said Mr. Matthews.

Jillian was leaning against his drawing board. She made a face at him. "Don't call me food-face."

"Why?" asked Mr. Matthews.

"It sounds gross," said Jillian, peeling a banana. "I don't like it."

"So tell me that," said Mr. Matthews, leaning back in his artist's chair and making it rock.

Jillian looked right at him. "Don't call me food-face, because I don't like it," she said.

"Please," said Mr. Matthews.

"Please," Jillian added.

"See?" said Mr. Matthews. "That wasn't so hard. And now I won't call you food-face anymore." He looked thoughtful. "You know, maybe sometime you'll want to say something like that to Mr. Granger."

Jillian stared at him, forgetting about the banana in her hand. Mr. Granger? Oh, no! It was easy to tell Daddy she didn't like being called food-face. But it would be hard to tell Mr. Granger she didn't like talking about shyness.

She remembered the banana in her hand and bit into it.

She was glad Daddy wasn't going to call her food-face anymore. He teased too much.

CHAPTER 12

The next day Mr. Moore's class had six cards on their balloon-ometer. Mrs. Hooper's class had five. But Miss Kraft's class had eight cards.

"We're ahead," yelled Ollie. "Like I told Mr. Granger, we're gonna win."

But the following day their class still had eight cards. So did Mr. Moore's class. But Mrs. Hooper's class was ahead with ten.

One or two cards came in the mail most days; the scores on the balloon-ometers rose slowly. Each class was in first place — for a while.

Some cards came right from town. People had found the balloons in their yards. And one had gone down on Fountain Square. But some cards came from farther away.

A trucker sent David's card. He had found it at a truck stop on the toll road.

A professor at a college found Elvis's card right outside her classroom window.

A farmer found Emmy's card in his cornfield. And a used-car salesman found Erin's card in his car lot.

But no card came for Jillian. She began to wonder if her balloon had gone down a tall smoke stack and got burned up. She held her breath each time Mrs. Perrin came to the door with mail.

One day Mrs. Perrin brought an envelope — just one — to the classroom. Jillian stared at it, making a wish. She crossed her fingers for luck.

Miss Kraft turned away from the door. She smiled at Jillian. "This one is for you," she said.

At last!

Jillian took the envelope. Why was her card

in an envelope? The person only had to put the card into the mail and not waste a stamp.

She looked closely at the postmark. "Detroit," she said. "That's where this card was mailed."

"That's the farthest-away place yet," said David as Jillian tore open the envelope.

Jillian took a sheet of folded paper out of the envelope. She looked in the envelope and shook it. Her card wasn't there. She unfolded the paper and squinted at it. On it was the most awful handwriting she had ever seen.

"Aren't you going to read it?" asked Emmy.

"We all read our cards out loud," said Erin.

Jillian frowned at the letter — for it was a letter. "This is really hard to read. I think it says, 'I looked this in the air one day.' Maybe I'm not reading it right."

"May I see it?" asked Miss Kraft.

Jillian gave her the letter.

"Mmm," said Miss Kraft. Her forehead wrinkled. "I give this person a Z in cursive writing."

Everyone giggled.

Miss Kraft went on. "It looks to me like it says, 'I hooked this in the air one day.' There's more. The writer printed it. Read it, Jillian."

Jillian read. " 'I'm big and I'm blue and I'd like to meet you.' Hey! That's a poem." She read on. " 'Tell me when, tell me where, and I'll be there.' He wrote his name. It's all squiggles. I think it says 'From . . . Blue . . . Rose . . .'?"

"Nobody has a name like that," said Elvis.

"That's a pretty terrible poem," said Courtney. Courtney wrote the best poems in their class.

"There's something more," said Jillian. She read slowly, " 'P.S. I'll need a big outdoor place where there's lots of space. Tell me where to come.' "

Everyone was silent. "It's a mystery," Elena whispered at last.

"May I see that again, Jillian?" asked Miss Kraft. She studied the letter some more. She looked puzzled and bit her lip. "How odd. It does look like his name is Blue Rose. And he does seem to want to come here. Oh, you and I will have to talk to Mr. Granger about that."

So then Miss Kraft told the class what pages

to work on in their workbooks. She made them promise not to get into an uproar while she went to the office with Jillian. "If I hear one word out in the hall. . . . " Her eyes got big. She leaned forward and whispered. "I won't tell you what Mr. Granger decides."

"Awwww. . . . "

She put her finger to her lips and the room was still.

Jillian looked back from the doorway. All she saw was the tops of heads of kids bent over their workbooks.

She hurried to catch up to Miss Kraft. Someone had found her balloon and that was good. But going to see Mr. Granger — that was terrible. Well, at least Miss Kraft was with her.

"Well, Miss Kraft." Mr. Granger's voice echoed off the walls. He looked down at Jillian. "Has our Jillian been misbehaving?"

Jillian's cheeks got warm. She looked at Mr. Granger's shoes. They were very big. She felt Miss Kraft's arm rest around her shoulders.

Miss Kraft laughed. "Why, Jillian wouldn't

misbehave. She's one of my best students."

The arm around Jillian's shoulders gave a little squeeze.

Quickly Miss Kraft told Mr. Granger about the letter.

"May I see it?" he asked. "Hmmm," he said as he read it. "Hmmm. Well. The balloon launch is, of course, a school project. Whatever we do about this we will all do together."

He thought some more and said "hmmm" some more. "Suppose we do it this way," he said at last. "Jillian, you write to this Mr., uh, Blue Rose. Thank him for writing to you. I will write to him, too, and find out more about this. Is that all right with you?"

Jillian thought that was just fine.

Mr. Granger wrote down the address on the envelope. Then Jillian and Miss Kraft went back to their room.

Miss Kraft stood for a minute with her hand on the doorknob. Not a sound came from inside the room. And so when they went inside, Miss Kraft told what Mr. Granger was going to do.

"This is very mysterious," said Elena.

"I love mysteries, too," said Erin.

Jillian wrote the letter right away.

Dear Mr. Blue Rose,

Thank you for writing to me. I am glad you found my balloon in Detroit. If Mr. Granger says it is okay, maybe you can come to see us. Why do you need a big outdoor place? Do not worry. I will find one.

Your friend,
Jillian Matthews

She wrote very carefully. She didn't want Mr. Blue Rose to have trouble reading her letter. She did not want to ever get a Z in cursive writing.

CHAPTER 13

Jillian could hardly wait to tell her father about Mr. Blue Rose. But Mr. Matthews wasn't home when she got there after school. Mrs. Matthews was.

The house smelled like a chocolate factory. Jillian sniffed the wonderful-smelling air and followed her nose to the kitchen.

Jackie was kneeling on a chair at the table, scraping a bowl. He had chocolate on his chin. "Want some?" he asked, holding out the spoon.

Jillian took a lick. "Yum-my! Thanks, Jack-O."

Two pans of brownies sat on the table. Two

whole panfuls. The brownies were cut into neat squares. "Can I have one?" she asked.

Mrs. Matthews was at the sink washing things. "*May* I have one. And don't I even get a hello?" she asked over her shoulder.

Jillian gave her a quick hug. "May I?" she asked. "There are almost enough brownies to last till Christmas."

"They aren't all for us," said Mrs. Matthews. "I'm taking some to school. It's Proud-of-Jason Day tomorrow." She smiled. "Jason talked today."

"You mean he really said a word?" asked Jillian. Her mother had been trying since school began to get Jason to talk.

Her mother laughed. "Not just one word. He said, 'I like the rabbit.' "

"A whole sentence! Wow!" said Jillian.

She slid a sideways look at her mother. "If I talk now, if I say a whole sentence now, may I have a brownie now?"

"Silly!" said her mother. "But they aren't quite ready. They need powdered sugar. Why don't you do that for me."

Jillian found a paper bag and put powdered

sugar in it. Then she shook the brownies in the bag, a few at a time. "Jackie got the bowl," she said, "so I guess I can eat the crumbs."

"But I shared," said Jackie.

Jillian let him help her eat the crumbs while she sugared the brownies.

Suddenly she remembered about Mr. Blue Rose. "I got a letter today," she said and told them all about it.

Mr. Matthews came in the back door while she was talking. He leaned his big, flat artist's case against the wall. "Did I hear you say Granger?" he asked. "Who came out ahead — you or him?"

Jillian skipped over that and told again all about the mysterious letter.

"Blue . . . Rose. . . ." Mr. Matthews's eyes had a faraway look. "Unusual. Detroit, you said. This Mr. B. Rose would be worth seeing, I think. Hey — aren't we going to sample those brownies?"

They each had a brownie — just one, so they wouldn't spoil their dinner. But Jerry didn't have any, because when he came in from basketball practice, dinner was ready.

Everyone was standing around the balloon-ometers when Jillian got to school the next morning.

"Ha-ha," said Jennifer Patimkin from Mr. Moore's room. "We're ahead."

Jillian hated people who said ha-ha.

"We'll bump you yet," said Ollie. "Wait and see. And anyway, ho-ho, we've got a mystery."

Jennifer and everyone in the hall looked envious. Nobody else in the whole school had a mystery to talk about.

After the bell rang and they all settled down in their seats, Miss Kraft wrote a name on the chalkboard: POLLY BUTTERMAN.

"A new girl will come into our class any day now. She's moving here from Minneapolis. I wonder. What can we do to make her feel welcome?"

"Draw pictures for her?" asked Jillian.

"Tell her jokes," said Elvis. "Like, why does the elephant wear pink ballet slippers?"

"Because — she — can't — dance — in — her — pink — tennis — shoes," everyone said in one voice.

"Aw, come on you guys," said Elvis. "Maybe she doesn't know that joke." His face lit up. "Maybe she'll know some new ones she can tell us."

"All right, people," said Miss Kraft. "Let's keep on track."

Emmy thought it would be a good idea to show the new girl where things were in Alcott School. "She can follow us to the learning center or the gym," she said. "But if she needs to go to the bathroom, and she's by herself, she won't know how to get there."

"We can put a sign on her desk that says, 'Hello, we're glad you are here,' " said Erin.

"Minneapolis," Nate said suddenly. "Hey — where's that?"

"In the United States, Dumbo," said Ollie.

Nate rolled his eyes. "I know that. I mean, where in the U.S.?"

David found it on the map. They spent a lot of time that day figuring out how far Minneapolis was from Evanston.

In the days that followed, a few more balloon cards came. And then there were none at all.

Mr. Moore's class and Miss Kraft's were neck and neck.

"I was sure we were going to win," said Ollie one morning as they trailed into their room after inspecting the balloon-ometers. He looked downhearted.

"I guess we'll get to keep the flag just half the time," said Courtney.

"That's not the same," said Nate.

It wasn't. They all agreed. Neck and neck definitely wasn't as good as being the only winner.

That very morning, Mrs. Perrin looked in at the door. Miss Kraft spoke to her quietly.

"Jillian," said Miss Kraft, turning back into the room, "Mr. Granger would like to talk to you."

Jillian's heart thunked down into her shoes.

"Come straight back," said Miss Kraft, "so we can talk about our reading project."

So Jillian had to go to see Mr. Granger. And Miss Kraft didn't even go with her.

CHAPTER
14

Jillian looked at her shoes all the way to the office. If only she were a bird — she could just fly away. But she wasn't a bird. She was herself, a girl named Jillian. She opened the door and went around Mrs. Perrin's desk and into Mr. Granger's office.

"Well, Jillian," Mr. Granger said in his superloud voice. "You will be interested to know I've just had a phone call from, uh, Blue Rose."

"You did?" Jillian was so interested that she peeked up at Mr. Granger. He was smiling.

"Miss Kraft tells me you're a good letter writer," said Mr. Granger.

It seemed kind of braggy to say yes. But since Miss Kraft had said so . . . Jillian nodded her head.

"It's time for you to invite Blue Rose to Lighthouse Park," said Mr. Granger.

What a good place! "It's big. It has lots of space, like Mr. Rose said in his letter," said Jillian, forgetting who she was talking to.

"Exactly," said Mr. Granger. "And we'll all be there — your class and Mrs. Hooper's and Mr. Moore's."

"The kids all think it's a mystery," said Jillian. "Now we're going to find out."

"We are indeed," said Mr. Granger. "So you may tell Blue Rose we'll be waiting in the park next Wednesday morning at nine o'clock."

Wait till the kids heard! Jillian started to leave. Then she remembered about being polite. "Thank you, Mr. Granger," she said.

"You're welcome," Mr. Granger boomed. Then he added, "You know, I think this really will be the year you overcome your shyness, Jillian."

Jillian was halfway to the door. She felt her face get hot. Why did Mr. Granger have to say that? Suddenly she could almost hear Daddy speaking. "Have you told. . . . "

She took a big breath and turned around. She looked right at Mr. Granger and said, "I don't like you to talk about shyness." Her voice was shaky. "Please don't. It makes me feel funny."

Mr. Granger's eyebrows went up. He blinked. When he spoke, his voice was softer, although it still rumbled. "Not another word," he promised. "Never again." He smiled. "Is it all right for me to say that took a lot of spunk? You're a brave girl, Jillian."

Jillian felt good. She felt full of bubbles. She smiled back at Mr. Granger. "Thanks, Mr. Granger."

She ran back to her room — even though running in the halls was not allowed. She felt as though she had wings. But she didn't want to use them to fly anywhere except back to class to tell everyone what was going to happen next week.

She wrote the letter that very afternoon.

Dear Mr. Blue Rose,

I am glad you are coming to see us. Everyone thinks you are a mystery. Please come to Lighthouse Park next Wednesday at nine o'clock. It is a pretty big place and has lots of space like you said in your letter. It is right on Sheridan Road. You will know you are there when you see the lighthouse and the flagpole and some really big rocks near the lake. Here is a map to help you find it. David made it.

Your friend,
Jillian Matthews

She drew a rose on the back of the envelope and colored it blue and wrote "Hi" next to it. She put the letter in the envelope and wrote the address on it and licked it shut.

Miss Kraft put a stamp on the letter and took it with her to mail after school.

Jillian walked home with Emmy and Erin.

"Miss Kraft had on that blue shirt today," said Erin, "and earrings. And she had blue stuff on her eyes. Maybe she's going to meet Mr. X after school."

"She wasn't all dressed up when I saw her at the Jewel that day," said Emmy. "She was wearing jeans and a sweatshirt."

"I went to the Jewel for my mom yesterday," said Jillian. "I looked near the fruit and vegetables. But Miss Kraft wasn't there. I mean, I thought maybe she would be."

They decided then and there to wait near the front entrance of Louisa May Alcott School every day to see if anybody came to pick up Miss Kraft. Anybody. They meant Mr. X.

Jillian flew straight upstairs to the studio as soon as she got into the house. Mr. Matthews was putting a blue wash on a piece of watercolor paper. She leaned against his drawing board, watching. The way the color spread out over the wet, white paper was a pretty thing to see.

"Dad, do you know what?" she asked.

"Sure do," said Mr. Matthews, tilting the paper so the color got darker at one side. "Haven't seen good old Ben What in weeks. How's he doing?"

"Oh, Daddy," said Jillian, "you're being silly. I mean, I did something today."

Mr. Matthews glanced at her. "Something good, I bet. Tell me."

Jillian told him about going to see Mr. Granger all by herself, and about Blue Rose coming, and —

Mr. Matthews interrupted her. "Now that is exciting. I may come to school to meet this Blue Rose, too."

"Do you mean it?" That would be neat. Fathers hardly ever came to school.

"Would I say it if I didn't mean it?" said Mr. Matthews.

"You'll have to come to the park, though," said Jillian, and she told him about that and writing the letter.

"There," said Mr. Matthews. He set the blue paper aside to dry.

"There's more," said Jillian. "Mr. Granger said that about shyness again."

Mr. Matthews leaned back in his chair. He didn't look at his paints or the watercolor paper. He just looked at Jillian. "Who won? The villain or you?"

"What's a villain?" asked Jillian.

"A bad guy," said Mr. Matthews.

"Oh." Jillian laughed. "I looked right at Mr. Granger and I asked him not to talk about shyness."

"You didn't!" said Mr. Matthews.

"I did!" Jillian said proudly. "And he said he would never talk about it again. And then he said I was brave to tell him that."

"You bet your best blue boots you were brave," said Mr. Matthews.

"I haven't got any blue boots," said Jillian.

"Beside the point," said Mr. Matthews. "Only you and I know that what you did took courage. My girl is one brave kid."

Jillian felt even nicer than the day she found she could stand up on ice skates and skim around on the ice. Suddenly she thought of something else.

"You know, Dad, Mr. Granger isn't a villain. He's really kind of nice."

"You don't say!" said Mr. Matthews, and he laughed.

CHAPTER 15

"Jilly! Look!" Emmy poked her. "It's him! Mr. X!"

Emmy was staring at the teachers standing near the fountain in Lighthouse Park. Jillian looked, too. A man was walking toward the teachers, and Miss Kraft was smiling at him.

"They've only got eyes for each other," sighed Erin.

"He's really good-looking," said Jillian, watching the man closely.

But then she was disappointed. Mr. X didn't hold Miss Kraft's hand or anything. He just stood around talking to everybody. If he was in love with Miss Kraft, wouldn't he hug her or something? Maybe this wasn't like *As the World Turns* after all.

She looked around, over the heads of all the kids jumping around the park. Where was Daddy? She had reminded him at breakfast that this was Blue Rose morning.

"What if old Blue Rose doesn't find us?" worried Nate.

"Sure he will," said David. "I draw pretty good maps."

Elvis seemed to have been thinking. "This guy wanted a really big place to come to. Maybe he's driving a semi."

Wow! Everybody liked that idea. They ran to the road and looked both ways, hoping to see a huge sixteen-wheeler coming toward them.

That's when Jillian saw her father. He crossed the road and came into the park. She ran to meet him, and she stood around while he said hello to Mr. Granger and the teachers, and they did all their grown-up talking.

Emmy and Erin came to stand with her so they could get a better look at Mr. X.

119

"He's wearing a sweatshirt," whispered Emmy. "Maybe he teaches phys ed."

Suddenly Erin gasped. "He just winked at Miss Kraft. I'm almost sure I saw him wink."

Jillian hadn't seen any wink. But maybe she had blinked and missed it.

Mr. Matthews turned to her at last. "I'm going to check out those boulders along the water," he said. "Want to come?"

Jillian did. So did Emmy and Erin — after they gave one last, long look at Mr. X.

The rocks were huge, just great for climbing. When Jillian got to the top of the biggest one, she was taller than her father. She looked down at the top of his head.

"Dad," she said, "did you know you've got a little hole in your hair on top?"

Mr. Matthews patted the top of his head and looked up at her. He rolled his eyes. "Let's keep it a secret between you and me, scout."

Jillian grinned at him. Then she turned around and around, looking, looking. Way out on the lake, where the water and the sky met in a hard, blue line, was a ship. She couldn't tell which way it was going, it moved so slowly. She stared, trying to figure it out.

And what was that? Something else was there. She squinched up her eyes to see better. It was above the water, so it wasn't a boat. And yet it didn't look like an airplane, either.

She pointed. "What's that?"

Mr. Matthews stared, too. "It's not like anything I've ever seen," he said.

Emmy and Erin sat down on the rock they had climbed. They leaned forward, trying to see better.

"It's not a bird . . . it's not a plane . . . it's not Superman," said Emmy.

"If it was a plane it would make noise," said Erin. "I don't hear anything."

Because Jillian and Emmy and Erin were all looking and pointing out over the lake, the kids waiting at the road came to find out what was happening.

"Is that the Goodyear blimp?" asked Elvis.

Jillian couldn't take her eyes off the strange thing that was coming nearer. "It's not the Goodyear blimp," she said, finally. The Goodyear blimp was shaped like a fat cigar. This did not have a cigar shape.

Everyone was quiet, watching.

"Is it blue?" Ollie asked after a while. "I think it's something blue."

Nobody answered.

"Why, it's . . . it's . . . a big hot-air balloon!" Jillian exclaimed at last. The balloon came nearer, nearer, drifting on the wind. And now she could see that it wasn't just round, with a basket hanging beneath it like the balloons she had seen on TV. This balloon had lumps and curves and ripples. It had a shape.

"It's a rose," Jillian breathed in wonder. "A big, blue rose."

The balloon seemed to fill the sky as it came close. It was going to fly almost overhead, kitty-corner across the park.

She scrambled down from her rock and ran to the playing field in the center of the park. Everyone followed her. They stood with their heads back, squinting up at the amazing sight, chattering.

"Hey! Will you look at that!"

"It's better than the Goodyear blimp."

"Wow! What makes it go?"

The enormous blue rose drifted overhead. It dipped, moving in over the autumn-tinted treetops. Someone was in the basket.

As Jillian watched, the pilot took off a safety helmet. Long copper-colored hair spilled over the pilot's shoulders. The pilot of the blue rose was a very pretty lady. She smiled and waved. The sun sparkled on her white teeth.

Everybody waved back and jumped up and down.

The lady leaned out of the basket and dropped something. A small parachute opened and carried a box downward. It landed on the grass.

But Jillian didn't pay any attention. Her eyes were on the big balloon. It dipped again, moved sideways, and then it rose and continued on its way, sailing up and over the trees on the far side of the park.

"Good-bye," Jillian called. "Good-bye, Blue Rose."

The Blue Rose disappeared beyond the trees.

She let out a long breath. Imagine! Blue Rose wasn't a man. Blue Rose wasn't even a woman. Blue Rose was a giant hot-air balloon!

"Hey, Jilly!" Ollie called. "That thing that came down — it has your name on it."

"What?" Jillian felt as though she were coming back to earth from a long adventure in another world. She looked around. "What?"

"The little parachute," called Emmy. "There's a box with it. Open it. Open it."

Mr. Granger was holding the box.

Jillian ran to him. Sure enough, the box did have her name on it.

She shook it. A tinny, cluttery rattle came from inside.

The box was tied up tight with string.

"Here. I've got a pocketknife," said Mr. Matthews. He snapped it open and cut the strings.

Jillian folded back the top of the box. The first thing she saw was a letter. She opened it, glad to see it was printed, and read:

Dear Jillian,

Your card floated near me one day when I was up in the Blue Rose. I hooked it right out of the air. Since the card came to me on a balloon, I thought it would be fun for a balloon to bring it back to you. So here we are.

I fooled you, letting you think you were writing to a person named Blue Rose. But come on now — isn't it fun to be fooled sometimes?

I am an artist. I make sky sculptures. The Blue Rose is my best. I hope you like it.

Sincerely,
Judy Blewrose

Fastened to the letter was Jillian's card, the one she had sent up with her pink balloon.

Nobody spoke for a minute. Then, "What's in that box?" asked Emmy.

Jillian jiggled it, looking into it. She reached in and held up a round pin with a picture of the Blue Rose on it. "There's a whole bunch of these," she said. "Maybe there's one for everybody."

"Neat-O!" yelled Ollie.

Everyone crowded around her, and soon everybody was wearing one of the Blue Rose pins.

Jillian looked down at the pin fastened to her sweater. She ran a finger over it. Judy Blewrose's Blue Rose had been a wonderful surprise. She was going to remember it forever and ever.

"Hey, you guys," called Nate.

Nobody heard him. They were all talking excitedly.

"HEY, EVERYBODY!" Nate roared.

The talking stopped. The kids turned to stare at him.

"Jillian got her card back," said Nate. The worry lines were gone from his face. He laughed. "Doesn't that mean our room wins the flag?"

It meant exactly that.

"We won," said Jillian, "by exactly one." She felt as light as — a hot-air balloon.

PART 3: Peanut Butter and Jelly

CHAPTER 16

The morning bell at Louisa May Alcott School jangled in a long peal of sound. Miss Kraft's students stood at their desks and said the Pledge of Allegiance. Then they settled down for the day. Everybody wore a round pin with a picture of the Blue Rose.

Some of the students had projects with the big dictionary. They were making lists of new words. Courtney had found some wonderful ones: "mythical" and "mystical" and "rune." She finished writing the words on her cards and went back to her desk to make sentences with them. Maybe she could even make a poem about a magician and runes.

Some of the students were working math problems Miss Kraft had written on the chalkboard. Nate was doing them very fast. But Emmy and Erin were chewing on their pencils and casting desperate looks at each other.

Some of the students were working with the big atlas. David was using his ruler to measure the distance from Detroit to Chicago. He was going to figure out exactly how far it was in miles.

At the front of the room, Jillian stood on a step stool at the board with her box of colored chalks. She was almost finished drawing a picture of the Blue Rose. She still needed to put dark shading on the undersides of the rose petals. And she was not happy with the color of Judy Blewrose's hair — it was too orange.

The classroom was a busy, quiet place.

Suddenly the door opened and Mrs. Perrin came in followed by a girl, a rather pudgy girl, with bright brown eyes and dark hair that rippled over her shoulders. She looked around the strange classroom eagerly, taking in the group at the dictionary, the group at the atlas, the colored leaves sandwiched between sheets of waxed paper and taped to the windows. Her dark eyes widened when she saw the drawing of the Blue Rose. Her mouth rounded into a surprised O.

Miss Kraft went to her. "You must be Polly," she said. "Come in." Her eyes lifted to the school secretary. "Thank you for bringing Polly to us, Mrs. Perrin," she said.

Mrs. Perrin left and Miss Kraft turned to the class. She took Polly's hand. "Class, this is Polly Butterman. I hope you will help her feel welcome."

Polly smiled. She felt awkward and strange with everybody staring at her.

Miss Kraft led her to a desk in the third row. "We've been expecting you, Polly, and some of the girls and boys wanted you to know we're glad to have you in our class. They fixed up your desk."

The desk was decorated with chains of colored paper rings. A sign on the seat said WELCOME. A bouquet of paper flowers was taped to the back of the seat. And there were things on top of the desk.

Polly forgot about feeling strange. "Wow!" she said without thinking about it. "This is neat!"

Everybody smiled, pleased that the new girl liked what they had done.

"Class," said Miss Kraft, "whatever you're doing, put it on hold. Return to your seats, and we'll tell Polly about ourselves, and she can tell us something about herself."

There was a general scramble as everyone sat down and put away notebooks and things.

Polly settled down at her new desk and looked at the things spread out on it. There were maps of the classroom and of the school and a pin with the picture of the hot-air flower balloon. She looked around. Everyone was wearing a pin-picture. She fastened hers to her sweater and looked at the other things on her desk. It was almost as good as a birthday party.

There was a poem about "Cheer" and "We are glad you are here," and a handmade book with a hand-drawn monster on the cover.

Monster Jokes was its title. She opened it to the first one:

Little Monster: Mommy, thank you for this delicious cookie. May I share it with my Monster friend?
Mother Monster: Stop behaving yourself this minute or I'm going to have to punish you.

Polly grinned. She did like jokes.

There was a watercolor picture of Louisa May Alcott School on the desk, too. It was a pretty good picture signed by someone named Jillian Matthews. Jillian — was that a girl's name or a boy's? Polly looked at the girl who had been drawing the hot-air flower balloon. Was she Jillian Matthews?

She remembered the drawing of the daisy she had brought to show her new classmates. She slipped it into her desk. Maybe she wouldn't show it to anyone after all. It wasn't nearly as good as the picture of the school.

There wasn't time to look at everything before the teacher asked everybody to stand up and say their names.

"My name is David," said a boy with so many freckles they almost ran together all over his face. "I made those maps for you. Now you won't get lost around here."

"My name is Courtney," said a girl with braids and glasses. "I wrote a poem for you. I rhymed Polly and holly. I wrote one about Polly and jolly, too, but I didn't give it to you because it was corny."

"I hope you like jokes," said a dark-haired boy. "And I hope you've got some new ones nobody's heard. I made the monster book for you." He sat down and popped up almost instantly. "Uh, my name is Elvis."

Emmy . . . Erin . . . Nate . . . Elena . . . Ollie . . . Allison . . . Kevin . . . Carrie . . . and more — one by one the girls and boys stood up and said their names. The last to speak was the girl with the blonde bangs and gray eyes who had been drawing the flower balloon.

She stood up and brushed her hand across her cheek, leaving a smear of blue chalk. "I'm Jillian," she said. Her voice was very soft. "Only everybody calls me Jilly. I made that picture of our school for you."

Miss Kraft came to stand beside Polly. "Would you like to tell us a little about yourself?" she asked.

Polly stood up and looked around at all the strange faces. She felt like the only marigold in a patch of petunias. Suddenly Miss Kraft's arm slipped around her shoulders and that made things better.

"My name is Polly Butterman," she said. "Only my friends call me Peanut. We used to live in Minneapolis. But my father died and we moved here — "

Elvis had a faraway look in his eyes. His lips were moving.

" — to be near my grandpa and grandma," Polly went on, "and because my mom is going back to college."

Elvis's eyes were darting from Polly to Jilly and back again.

Polly continued. "On our way here we found a puppy that was starving." She held up a picture of Nibbsie. "He had a broken leg and we took him to a vet and he's got a cast on his leg, but now he's my — "

"Peanut Butterman and — " Elvis burst out. Everyone stared at him.

" — and Jilly!" Elvis almost choked, laughing. "We've got Peanut butter and Jilly in this room."

Laughter rippled around the room.

Elvis's face was red. "Peanut butter and jelly!" he giggled, pointing from Polly to Jillian. He slapped his knee. "That's the funniest thing I ever heard!"

Elvis's giggling was catching. The laughter in the room got louder.

"All right now, Elvis," said Miss Kraft, "don't go off into one of your giggling fits." But her lips were quirking upward, too.

Nothing could stop Elvis once he started to laugh. He leaned back in his seat, his hands on his sides, his head back, guffawing, gasping, "Peanut butter and jelly!"

Polly had to giggle. It did sound silly — Peanut butter and jelly. She looked across the rows at the girl with gray eyes and blonde bangs. That Jilly did look awfully quiet. Was she any fun?

Pink-cheeked, but laughing, Jillian looked back at Polly. What was this new girl like? Was she going to be nice to know?

Polly and Jillian stared at each other, wondering . . . wondering. . . .